Oliver Wendell Holmes

Mechanism in thought and morals:

An address delivered before the Phi Beta Kappa Society of Harvard

University, June 29, 1870, with notes and after-thoughts. Fourth Edition

Oliver Wendell Holmes

Mechanism in thought and morals:
An address delivered before the Phi Beta Kappa Society of Harvard University, June 29, 1870, with notes and after-thoughts. Fourth Edition

ISBN/EAN: 9783337872724

Printed in Europe, USA, Canada, Australia, Japan

Cover: Foto ©Andreas Hilbeck / pixelio.de

More available books at **www.hansebooks.com**

MECHANISM

IN

THOUGHT AND MORALS.

AN ADDRESS

DELIVERED BEFORE THE PHI BETA KAPPA SOCIETY OF
HARVARD UNIVERSITY, JUNE 29, 1870.

WITH NOTES AND AFTERTHOUGHTS.

BY

OLIVER WENDELL HOLMES

FOURTH EDITION.

"Car il ne faut pas se méconnaître, nous sommes automates autant
qu'esprit." — PASCAL: *Pensées*, chap. xi. § 4.

BOSTON:

JAMES R. OSGOOD & CO.,
LATE TICKNOR & FIELDS, AND FIELDS, OSGOOD, & CO.
1877.

Boston:
Stereotyped and Printed by Rand, Avery, & Frye.

INTRODUCTION.

It is fair to claim for this Essay the license which belongs to all spoken addresses. To hold the attention of an audience is the first requisite of every such composition; and for this a more highly colored rhetoric is admissible than might please the solitary reader. The check of a stage heroine will bear a touch of carmine which would hardly improve the sober comeliness of the mother of a family at her fireside.

So too, on public occasions, a wide range of suggestive inquiry, meant to stimulate rather than satiate the interest of the listeners, ma., with some reason, be preferred to that more complete treatment of a narrowly limited subject which is liable to prove exhaustive in a double sense.

In the numerous notes and other additions, I have felt the right to use a freedom of expression which some might think out of place before the mixed audience of a literary anniversary. The dissentient listener may find himself in an uneasy position hard to escape from : the dissatisfied reader has an easy remedy.

MECHANISM

IN

THOUGHT AND MORALS.

A S the midnight train rolls into an inter-
mediate station, the conductor's voice
is heard announcing, "Cars stop ten minutes
for refreshments." The passengers snatch a
brief repast, and go back, refreshed, we will
hope, to their places. But, while they are at
the tables, one may be seen going round
among the cars with a lantern and a hammer, intent upon a graver business. He is
clinking the wheels to try if they are sound.
His task is a humble and simple one: he is
no machinist, very probably; but he can cast
a ray of light from his lantern, and bring out
the ring of iron with a tap of his hammer.

Our literary train is stopping for a very brief time at its annual station; and I doubt not it will be refreshed by my youthful colleague before it moves on. It is not unlikely the passengers may stand much in need of refreshment before I have done with them: for I am the one with the hammer and the lantern; and I am going to clink some of the wheels of this intellectual machinery, on the soundness of which we all depend. The slenderest glimmer I can lend, the lightest blow I can strike, may at least call the attention of abler and better-equipped inspectors.

I ask your attention to some considerations on the true mechanical relations of the thinking principle, and to a few hints as to the false mechanical relations which have intruded themselves into the sphere of moral self-determination.

I call that part of mental and bodily life mechanical which is independent of our volition. The beating of our hearts and the secretions of our internal organs will go on, without and in spite of any voluntary effort of ours, as long as we live. Respiration is partially under our control : we can change the rate and special mode of breathing, and even hold our breath for a time ; but the most determined suicide cannot strangle him- · self without the aid of a noose or other contrivance which shall effect what his mere will cannot do. The flow of thought is, like breathing, essentially mechanical and necessary, but incidentally capable of being modified to a greater or less extent by conscious effort. Our natural instincts and tastes have a basis which can no more be reached by the will than the sense of light and darkness, or that of heat and cold. All these things we feel justified in referring to the great First Cause : they belong to the " laws of Nature," as we call them, for which we are not accountable.

Whatever may be our opinions as to the relations between "mind" and "matter," our observation only extends to thought and emotion as connected with the living body, and, according to the general verdict of consciousness, more especially with certain parts of the body; namely, the central organs of the nervous system. The bold language of certain speculative men of science has frightened some more cautious persons away from a subject as much belonging to natural history as the study of any other function in connection with its special organ. If Mr. Huxley maintains that his thoughts and ours are "the expression of molecular changes in that matter of life which is the source of our other vital phenomena;"[1] if the Rev. Prof. Haughton suggests, though in the most guarded way, that "our successors may even dare to speculate on the changes that converted a crust of bread, or a bottle of wine, in the brain of Swift, Molière, or Shakspeare, into the conception of the gentle Glumdalclitch, the rascally Sganarelle, or the immortal Falstaff,"[2] — all this need not

---

[1] On the Physical Basis of Life. New Haven, 1870, p. 261.

[2] Medicine in Modern Times. London, 1869, p. 107.

frighten us from studying the conditions of the thinking organ in connection with thought, just as we study the eye in its relations to sight. The brain, is an instrument, necessary, so far as our direct observation extends, to thought. The "materialist" believes it to be wound up by the ordinary cosmic forces, and to give them out again as mental products:[1] the "spiritualist" believes in a conscious entity, not interchangeable with motive force, which plays upon this instrument. But the instrument must be studied by the one as much as by the other: the piano which the master touches must be as thoroughly understood as the musical box or clock which goes of itself by a spring or weight.. A slight congestion or softening of the brain shows the least materialistic of

---

[1] "It is by no means generally admitted that the brain is governed by the mind. On the contrary, the view entertained by the best cerebral physiologists is, that the mind is a force developed by the action of the brain." — *Journal of Psychological Medicine,* July, 1870; Editor's (W. A. Hammond) *Note,* p. 535.

philosophers that he must recognize the strict
dependence of mind upon its organ in the
only condition of life with which we are
experimentally acquainted. And what all
recognize as soon as disease forces it upon
their attention, all thinkers should recognize,
without waiting for such an irresistible
demonstration. They should see that the
study of the organ of thought, microscopi-
cally, chemically, experimentally, on the
lower animals, in individuals and races, in
health and in disease, in every aspect of
external observation, as well as by internal
consciousness, is just as necessary as if mind
were known to be nothing more than a
function of the brain, in the same way as
digestion is of the stomach.

These explanations are simply a concession
to the timidity of those who assume that
they who study the material conditions of
the thinking centre necessarily confine the
sphere of intelligence to the changes in those
conditions ; that they consider these changes
constitute thought; whereas all that is held

may be, that they accompany thought. It
is a well-ascertained fact, for instance, that
certain sulphates and phosphates are separated from the blood that goes to the brain
in increased quantity after severe mental
labor. But this chemical change may be
only one of the factors of intellectual action.
So, also, it *may* be true that the brain is inscribed with material records of thought; but
what that is which reads any such records,
remains still an open question. I have meant
to leave absolutely untouched the endless dis-
cussion as to the distinctions between " mind "
and " matter," [1] and confine myself chiefly to
some results of observation in the sphere of
thought, and some suggestions as to the
mental confusion which seems to me a common fact in the sphere of morals.

The central thinking organ is made up of
a vast number of little starlike bodies embed-

---

[1] Matter itself has been called "frozen force,"
and, as Boscovich has said, is only known to us as
localized points of attraction and repulsion.

ded in fine granular matter, connected with each other by ray-like branches in the form of pellucid threads; the same which, wrapped in bundles, become nerves, — the telegraphic cords of the system. The brain proper is a double organ, like that of vision; its two halves being connected by a strong transverse band, which unites them like the Siamese twins. The most fastidious lover of knowledge may study its general aspect as an after-dinner amusement upon an English walnut, splitting it through its natural suture, and examining either half. The resemblance is a curious freak of Nature's, which Cowley has followed out, in his ingenious, whimsical way, in his fifth " Book of Plants ; " thus rendered in the old translation from his original Latin : —

> " Nor can this head-like nut, shaped like the brain
> Within, be said that form by chance to gain :
> For membranes soft as silk her kernel bind,
> Whereof the inmost is of tenderest kind,
> Like those which on the brain of man we find;
> All which are in a seam-joined shell enclosed,
> Which of this brain the skull may be supposed."

The brain must be fed, or it cannot work. Four great vessels flood every part of it with hot scarlet blood, which carries at once fire and fuel to each of its atoms. Stop this supply, and we drop senseless. Inhale a few whiffs of ether, and we cross over into the unknown world of death with a return-ticket; or we prefer chloroform, and perhaps get no return-ticket. Infuse a few drachms of another fluid into the system, and, when it mounts from the stomach to the brain, the pessimist becomes an optimist; the despairing wretch finds a new heaven and a new earth, and laughs and weeps by turns in his brief ecstasy. But, so long as a sound brain is supplied with fresh blood, it perceives, thinks, wills.[1] The father of Eugène Sue, the novelist in a former generation, and M. Pinel in this, and very recently, have advocated doing

---

[1] That is, acts as the immediate instrument through which these phenomena are manifested. So a good watch, in good order and wound up, tells us the time of day. The making and winding-up forces remain to be accounted for.

away with the guillotine, on the ground that
the man, or the nobler section of him, might
be conscious for a time after the axe had
fallen.   We need not believe it, nor the story
of Charlotte Corday; still less that one of
Sir Everard Digby, that when the execu-
tioner held up his heart to the gaze of the
multitude, saying, " This is the heart of a
traitor!" the severed head exclaimed, " Thou
liest ! "   These stories show, however, the
sense we have that our personality is seated
in the great nervous centre ; and, if physiologists could experiment on human beings as
some of them have done on animals, I will
content myself with hinting that they would
have tales to relate which would almost rival
the legend of St. Denis.[1]

---

[1] There is a ghastly literature of the axe and
block, of which the stories above referred to are
specimens.   All the express trials made on the
spot after executions in 1803, in 1853, and more
recently at Beauvais, have afforded only negative
results, as might be anticipated from the fact
that the circulation through the brain is instantly

An abundant supply of blood to a part implies a great activity in its functions. The oxygen of the blood keeps the brain in a continual state of spontaneous combustion. The waste of the organ implies as constant a repair. " Every meal is a rescue from one death, and lays up for another; and, while we think a thought, we die," says Jeremy Taylor. It is true of the brain as of other organs : it can only live by dying. We must all be born again, atom by atom, from hour to hour, or perish all at once beyond repair.[1]

---

arrested; and Père Duchesne's *éternuer dans le sac* must pass as a frightful pleasantry. But a distinguished physiological experimenter informed me that the separated head of a dog, on being injected with fresh blood, manifested signs of life and intelligence. — See *London Quarterly Review*, vol. lxxiii. p. 273 *et seq.;* also *N. Y. Medical Gazette* for April 9, 1870. The reader who would compare Dr. Johnson's opinion of vivisection with Mr. Huxley's recent defence of it may consult the *Idler*, No. 17.

[1] It is proper to say here, that the waste occur-

Such is the aspect, seen in a brief glance, of the great nervous centre. It is constantly receiving messages from the senses, and transmitting orders to the different organs by the " up and down trains " of the nervous influence. It is traversed by continuous lines of thought, linked together in sequences which are classified under the name of "laws of association." The movement of these successions of thought is so far a result of mechanism, that, though we may modify them by an exertion of will, we cannot stop them, and remain vacant of all ideas.

My bucolic friends tell me that our horned cattle always keep a cud in their mouths: when they swallow one, another immediately replaces it. If the creature happens to lose

---

ring in an organ is by no means necessarily confined to its stationary elements. The blood itself in the organ, and for the time constituting a part of it, appears to furnish the larger portion of the fuel, if we may call it so, which is acted on by its own oxygen. This, at least, is the case with muscle; and is probably so elsewhere.

its cud, it must have an artificial one given it, or, they assure me, it will pine, and perhaps die. Without committing myself to the exactness or the interpretation of the statement, I may use it as an illustration. Just in the same way, one thought replaces another; and in the same way the mental cud is sometimes lost while one is talking, and he must ask his companion to supply its place. "What was I saying?" we ask; and our friend furnishes us with the lost word or its equivalent, and the jaws of conversation begin grinding again.

The brain being a double organ, like the eye, we naturally ask whether we can think with one side of it, as we can see with one eye; whether the two sides commonly work together; whether one side may not be stronger than the other; whether one side may not be healthy, and the other diseased; and what consequences may follow from these various conditions. This is the subject ingeniously treated by Dr. Wigan in his work on the duality of the mind. He

2

maintains and illustrates by striking facts the
independence of the two sides ; which, so far
as headache is concerned, many of my audience must know from their own experience.
The left half of the brain, which controls
the right half of the body, is, he believes, the
strongest in all but left-handed persons.[1]

The resemblance of the act of intelligence
to that of vision is remarkably shown in the
terms we borrow from one to describe the
other.   We *see* a truth ; we *throw light* on a
subject; we *elucidate* a proposition ; we *darken*

---

[1] Gratiolet states that the left frontal convolutions are developed earlier than the right.   Baillarger attributes right-handedness to the better
nutrition of the left hemisphere, in consequence
of the disposition of the arteries; Hyrtl, to the
larger current of blood to the right arm, &c. — See
an essay on "Right and Left Handedness," in the
Journal of Psychological Medicine for July, 1870,
by Thomas Dwight, jun., M.D. ; also "Aphasia and
the Physiology of Speech," by T. W. Fisher, in the
Boston Medical and Surgical Journal for Sept. 22,
1870.

counsel ; we are *blinded* by prejudice ; we take a *narrow view* of things; we look at our neighbor with a *jaundiced eye.* These are familiar expressions; but we can go much farther. We have intellectual myopes, near-sighted specialists, and philosophers who are purblind to all but the distant abstract. We have judicial intellects as nearly achromatic as the organ of vision, eyes that are color-blind, and minds that seem hardly to have the sense of beauty. The old brain thinks the world grows worse, as the old retina thinks the eyes of needles and the fractions in the printed sales of stocks grow smaller. Just as the eye seeks to refresh itself by resting on neutral tints after looking at brilliant colors, the mind turns from the glare of intellectual brilliancy to the solace of gentle dulness; the tranquillizing green of the sweet human qualities, which do not make us shade our eyes like the spangles of conversational gymnasts and figurantes.

We have a field of vision : have we a field of thought ? Before referring to some matters of individual experience, I would avail myself of Sir John Herschel's apology, that the nature of the subject renders such reference inevitable; as it is one that can only be elucidated by the individual's putting on record his own personal contribution to the stock of facts accumulating.

Our conscious mental action, aside from immediate impressions on the senses, is mainly pictured, worded, or modulated, as in remembered music; all, more or less, under the influence of the will. In a general way, we refer the seat of thinking to the anterior part of the head. *Pictured* thought is in relation with the field of vision, which I perceive — as others do, no doubt — as a transverse ellipse; its vertical to its horizontal diameter about as one to three. We shut our eyes to recall a visible object: we see visions by night. The bright ellipse becomes a black ground, on which ideal images show more distinctly than on the illuminated one. The form of the mental field of vision is illustrated by the fact, that we can follow in our idea a ship sailing, or a horse running, much farther, without a sense of effort, thàn we can a balloon rising. In seeing persons, this field of mental vision seems to be a little in front of the eyes. Dr. Howe kindly answers a letter of inquiry as follows : —

" Most congenitally-blind persons, when asked with what part of the brain they think, answer, that they are not conscious of having any brain.

" I have asked several of the most thoughtful and intelligent among our pupils to designate, as nearly as they can, the seat of sensation in thought ; and they do so by placing the hand upon the *anterior* and *upper* part of the cranium."

Worded thought is attended with a distinct impulse towards the organs of speech : in fact, the effort often goes so far, that we " think aloud," as we say.[1]   The seat of

---

[1] The greater number of readers are probably in the habit of articulating the words mentally. Beginners read syllable by syllable.

" A man must be a poor beast," said Dr. John-

this form of mental action seems to me to be beneath that of pictured thought; indeed, to follow certain nerves downward : so that, as we say, " My heart was in my mouth,"

---

son, " that should read no more in quantity than he could utter aloud." There are books of which we can exhaust a page of its meaning at a glance ; but a man cannot do justice to a poem like Gray's Elegy except by the distinct mental articulation of every word. Some persons read sentences and paragraphs as children read syllables ; taking their sense in block, as it were. All instructors who have had occasion to consult a text-book at the last moment before entering the lecture-room know that *clairvoyant* state well enough in which a page prints itself on their perception as the form of types stamped itself on the page.

We can read aloud, or mentally articulate, and keep up a distinct train of pictured thought, — not so easily two currents of worded thought simultaneously: though this can be done to some extent; as, for instance, one may be reading aloud, and internally articulating some well-known passage.

we could almost say, "My brain is my mouth." A particular spot has been of late pointed out by pathologists, not phrenologists, as the seat of the faculty of speech.[1] I do know that our sensations ever point to it. *Modulated* or musical consciousness is to pictured and worded thought as algebra is to geometry and arithmetic. Music has an absolute sensuous significance — the wood-chuck which used to listen to my friend playing the piano I suppose stopped at that;[2] — but for human beings it does not cause a mere sensation, nor an emotion, nor a definable intellectual state, though it may excite many various emotions and trains of worded or pictured thought. But words cannot truly define it: we might as well give a man a

---

[1] A part of the left anterior lobe. — See Dr. Fisher's elaborate paper before referred to.

[2] For various alleged instances of the power of music over different lower animals, — the cow, the stag, mice, serpents, spiders, — see Dwight's *Journal of Music* for Oct. 26, 1861.

fiddle, and tell him to play the Ten Command-
ments, as give him a dictionary, and tell him
to describe the music of " Don Giovanni."

The nerves of hearing clasp the roots of
the brain as a creeping vine clings to the
bole of an elm.   The primary seat of musical
consciousness seems to be behind and below
that of worded thought; but it radiates in all
directions, calling up pictures and words, as
I have said, in endless variety.   Indeed, the
various mental conditions I have described
are so frequently combined, that it takes
some trouble to determine the locality of
each.

The seat of the *will* seems to vary with
the organ through which it is manifested;
to transport itself to different parts of the
brain, as we may wish to recall a picture,
a phrase, or a melody; to throw its force
on the muscles or the intellectual processes.
Like the general-in-chief, its place is any-
where in the field of action.   It is the least
like an instrument of any of our faculties;
the farthest removed from our conceptions of

mechanism and matter, as we commonly define them.

This is my parsimonious contribution to our knowledge of the relations existing between mental action and space. Others may have had a different experience; the great apostle did not know at one time whether he was in the body or out of the body: but my system of phrenology extends little beyond this rudimentary testimony of consciousness.

When it comes to the relation of mental action and *time*, we can say with Leibnitz, "*Calculemus;*" for here we can reach quantitative results. The "personal equation," or difference in rapidity of recording the same occurrence, has been recognized in astronomical records since the time of Maskelyne, the royal astronomer; and is allowed for with the greatest nicety, as may be seen, for instance, in Dr. Gould's recent report on Transatlantic Longitude. More recently, the time required in mental processes and in the transmission of sensation and the motor impulse along nerves has been carefully studied by Helmholtz, Fizeau, Marey, Donders, and others.[1] From forty to eighty, a hundred or more feet a second are estimates of different observers: so that, as the newspapers have been repeating, it would take a whale a second, more or less, to feel the stroke of a harpoon in his tail.[2] Compare this with the velocity of galvanic signals, which Dr. Gould

---

[1] See *Annual of Scientific Discovery* for 1851, 1858, 1863, 1866; *Journal of Anatomy and Physiology*, 2d Series, No. 1, for November, 1867; MAREY, *Du Mouvement dans les Fonctions de la Vie*, p. 430 *et seq.*

[2] Mr. W. F. Barrett calculates, that as the mind requires one-tenth of a second to form a conception and act accordingly, and as a rifle-bullet would require no more than one-thousandth of a second to pass through the brain, it could not be felt (*An. Sc. Discov.*, 1866–7, p. 278). When Charles XII. was struck dead by the cannon-ball, he clapped his hand on his sword. This, however, may have probably been an unconscious reflex action.

has found to be from fourteen to eighteen thousand miles a second through iron wire on poles, and about sixty-seven hundred miles a second through the submarine cable. The brain, according to Fizeau, takes one-tenth of a second to transmit an order to the muscles; and the muscles take one-hundredth of a second in getting into motion. These results, such as they are, have been arrived at by experiments on single individuals with a very delicate chronometric apparatus. I have myself instituted a good many experiments with a more extensive and expensive machinery than I think has ever been employed, — namely, two classes, each of ten intelligent students, who with joined hands represented a nervous circle of about sixty-six feet: so that a hand-pressure transmitted ten times round the circle traversed six hundred and sixty feet, besides involving one hundred perceptions and volitions. My chronometer was a " horse-timer," marking quarter-seconds. After some practice, my second class gradually reduced the time of transmission ten times round, which, like that of the first class, had stood at fourteen and fifteen seconds, down to ten seconds; that is, one-tenth of a second for the passage through the nerves and brain of each individual, — less than the least time I have ever seen assigned for the whole operation; no more than Fizeau has assigned to the action of the brain alone. The mental process of judgment between colors (red, white, and green counters), between rough and smooth (common paper and sand-paper), between smells (camphor, cloves, and assafœtida), took about three and a half tenths of a second each; taste, twice or three times as long, on account of the time required to reach the true sentient portion of the tongue.[1] These few results of my numerous experiments show the rate of working of the different

---

[1] Some of these results assign a longer time than other observers have found to be required. A little practice would materially shorten the time, as it did in the other experiment.

parts of the machinery of consciousness. Nothing could be easier than to calculate the whole number of perceptions and ideas a man could have in the course of a lifetime.[1]

---

[1] "The sensible points of the retina, according to Weber and Smith, measure no more than the $\frac{1}{8000}$ inch in diameter. If, adopting the views of Mr. Solly, we consider the convolutions of the brain as made up of an extensive surface of cineritious neurine, we may estimate the number of ideas, the substrata of which may be contained in a square inch, as not certainly less than 8,000; and, as there must be an immense number of square inches of surface in the gray matter extended through the cerebro-spinal axis of man, there is space sufficient for millions." — *On the Reflex Function of the Brain,* by T. LAYCOCK, M.D. *Brit. and For. Med. Review* for January, 1845.

Dr. Hooke, the famous English mathematician and philosopher, made a calculation of the number of separate ideas the mind is capable of entertaining, which he estimated as 3,155,760,000. — HALLER: *Elementa Physiologiæ,* vol. v. p. 547. The nerve-cells of the brain vary in size from $\frac{1}{3000}$ to $\frac{1}{300}$ of an inch in diameter (MARSHALL's *Physiol-*

But as we think the same thing over many
millions of times, and as many persons keep
up their social relations by the aid of a vocabulary of only a few hundred words, or,
in the case of some very fashionable people,
a few scores only, a very limited amount of
thinking material may correspond to a full
set of organs of sense, and a good development of the muscular system.[1]

---

ogy, i. 77) ; and the surface of the convolutions is
reckoned by Baillarger at about 670 square inches
(*ibid.*, p. 302) ; which, with a depth of one-fifth of
an inch, would give 134 cubic inches of cortical
substance, and, if the cells average $\frac{1}{1000}$ of an inch,
would allow room in the convolutions for 134,000,-
000,000 cells. But they are mingled with white
nerve-fibres and granules. While these calcula-
tions illustrate the extreme complexity of the
brain-substance, they are amusing rather than ex-
planatory of mental phenomena, and belong to
the province of *Science mousseuse*, to use the
lively expression of a French academician at a
recent session.

[1] The use of *slang*, or cheap generic terms, as a

The time-relation of the sense of vision was illustrated by Newton by the familiar

---

substitute for differentiated specific expressions, is at once a sign and a cause of mental atrophy. It is the way in which a lazy adult shifts the trouble of finding any exact meaning in his (or her) conversation on the other party. If both talkers are indolent, all their talk lapses into the vague generalities of early childhood, with the disadvantage of a vulgar phraseology. It is a prevalent social vice of the time, as it has been of times that are past.

"Thus has he (and many more of the same breed, that, I know, the drossy age dotes on) only got the tune of the time, and outward habit of encounter; a kind of yesty collection, which carries them through and through the most fond and winnowed opinions; and, do but blow them to their trial, the bubbles are out." — *Hamlet,* act v. sc. 2.

Swift says (in the character of Simon Wagstaff, Esq.), speaking of "witty sentences," "For, as long as my memory reaches, I do not recollect one new phrase of importance to have been added; which defect in us moderns I take to have been occasioned by the introduction of cant-words in

experiment of whirling a burning brand, which appears as a circle of fire. The duration of *associated* impressions on the memory differs vastly, as we all know, in different individuals. But, in uttering distinctly a series of unconnected numbers or letters before a succession of careful listeners, I have been surprised to find how generally they break down, in trying to repeat them. between seven and ten figures or letters; though here and there an individual may be depended on for a larger number. Pepys mentions a person who could repeat sixty unconnected words, forwards or backwards, and perform other wonderful feats of mem-

---

the reign of King CHARLES the Second." — *A Complete Collection of Genteel and Ingenious Conversation*, &c. Introduction.

"English is an expressive language," said Mr. Pinto, "but not difficult to master. Its range is limited. It consists, as far as I can observe, of four words, — 'nice,' 'jolly,' 'charming,' and 'bore;' and some grammarians add 'fond.'" — *Lothair*, chap. xxviii.

ory; but this was a prodigy.[1] I suspect we have in this and similar trials a very simple mental dynamometer which may yet find its place in education.

Do we ever think without knowing that we are thinking? The question may be disguised so as to look a little less paradoxical. Are there any mental processes of which we are unconscious at the time, but which we recognize as having taken place by finding certain results in our minds?[2]

That there are such unconscious mental actions is laid down in the strongest terms

---

[1] This is nothing to the story told by Seneca of himself, and still more of a friend of his, one Portius *Latro* (*Mendax*, it might be suggested); or to that other relation of Muretus about a certain young Corsican. — See REES's *Cyclopædia*, art. *Memory;* also HALLER's *Elem. Phys.*, v. 548, &c.

[2] " Such a process of reasoning is more or less implicit, and *without the direct and full advertence of the mind exercising it.*" — J. H. NEWMAN: *Essay in Aid of a Grammar of Assent.*

by Leibnitz, whose doctrine reverses the axiom of Descartes into *sum, ergo cogito.* The existence of unconscious thought is maintained by him in terms we might fairly call audacious, and illustrated by some of the most striking facts bearing upon it. The " insensible perceptions," he says, are as important in pneumatology as corpuscles are in physics. — It does not follow, he says again, that, because we do not perceive thought, it does not exist. — Something goes on in the mind which answers to the circulation of the blood and all the internal movements of the viscera. — In one word, it is a great source of error to believe that there is no perception in the mind but those of which it is conscious. —

This is surely a sufficiently explicit and peremptory statement of the doctrine, which, under the names of " latent consciousness," " obscure perceptions," " the hidden soul," " unconscious cerebration," " reflex action of the brain," has been of late years emerging into general recognition in treatises of psychology and physiology.

His allusion to the circulation of the blood and the movements of the viscera, as illustrating his paradox of thinking without knowing it, shows that he saw the whole analogy of the mysterious intellectual movement with that series of reflex actions so fully described half a century later by Hartley, whose observations, obscured by wrong interpretation of the cerebral structure, and an insufficient theory of vibrations which he borrowed from Newton, are yet a remarkable anticipation of many of the ideas of modern physiology, for which credit has been given so liberally to Unzer and Prochaska. Unconscious activity is the rule with the actions most important to life. The lout who lies stretched on the tavern-bench, with just mental activity enough to keep his pipe from going out, is the unconscious tenant of a laboratory where such combinations are being constantly made as never Wöhler or Berthelot could put together; where such fabrics are woven, such colors dyed, such problems of mechanism solved, such a commerce carried on with the elements and forces of the outer universe, that the industries of all the factories and trading establishments in the world are mere indolence and awkwardness and unproductiveness compared to the miraculous activities of which his lazy bulk is the unheeding centre. All these unconscious or reflex actions take place by a mechanism never more simply stated than in the words of Hartley, as " *vibrations* which ascend up the sensory nerves first, and then are detached down the motory nerves, which communicate with these by some common trunk, plexus, or ganglion." [1]

---

[1] He goes on to draw the distinction between " automatic motions of the secondary kind " and those which were originally automatic. " The fingers of young children bend upon almost every impression which is made upon the palm of the hand; thus performing the action of grasping in the original automatic manner." ("He rastled with my finger, the blank little etc. !" says the hard-swearing but tender-hearted " Kentuck," speaking of the new-born babe whose story Mr. Harte has told so touchingly in " The Luck of

The doctrine of Leibnitz, that the brain may sometimes act without our taking cognizance of it, as the heart commonly does, as many internal organs always do, seems almost to belong to our time. The readers of Hamilton and Mill, of Abercrombie, Laycock, and Maudsley, of Sir John Herschel, of Carpenter, of Lecky, of Dallas, will find many variations on the text of Leibnitz, some new illustrations, a new classification and nomenclature of the facts; but the root of the matter is all to be found in his writings.

Roaring Camp.") Hartley traces this familiar nursery experience onwards, until the original automatic action becomes associated with sensations and ideas, and by and by subject to the will; and shows still further how this and similar actions, by innumerable repetitions, reach another stage, "repassing through the same degrees in an inverted order, till they become secondarily automatic on many ocasions, though still perfectly voluntary on some; viz., whensoever an express act of the will is exerted." — *Obs. on Man: Propositions* xix. xxi.

I will give some instances of work done in the underground workshop of thought, — some of them familiar to the readers of the authors just mentioned.

We wish to remember something in the course of conversation. No effort of the will can reach it; but we say, " Wait a minute, and it will come to me," and go on talking. Presently, perhaps some minutes later, the idea we are in search of comes all at once into the mind, delivered like a prepaid bundle, laid at the door of consciousness like a foundling in a basket. How it came there we know not. The mind must have been at work groping and feeling for it in the dark : it cannot have come of itself. Yet, all the while, our consciousness, so far as we are conscious of our consciousness, was busy with other thoughts.

In old persons, there is sometimes a long interval of obscure mental action before the answer to a question is evolved. I remember making an inquiry, of an ancient man whom I met on the road in a wagon with his daughter, about a certain old burial-ground which I was visiting. He seemed to listen attentively ; but I got no answer. " Wait half a minute or so," the daughter said, " and he will tell you." And sure enough, after a little time, he answered me, and to the point. The delay here, probably, corresponded to what machinists call " lost time," or " back lash," in turning an old screw, the thread of which is worn. But, within a fortnight, I examined a young man for his degree, in whom I noticed a certain regular interval, and a pretty long one, between every question and its answer. Yet the answer was, in almost every instance, correct, when at last it did come. It was an idiosyncrasy, I found, which his previous instructors had noticed. I do not think the mind knows what it is doing in the interval, in such cases. This latent period, during which the brain is obscurely at work, may, perhaps, belong to mathematicians more than others. Swift said of Sir Isaac Newton, that, if one were to ask him a question, " he would revolve it in a circle in his brain, round and round and round" (the narrator here describing a circle on his own forehead), "before he could produce an answer."[1]

I have often spoken of the same trait in a distinguished friend of my own, remarkable for hi. mathematical genius, and compared his sometimes long-deferred answer to a question, with half a dozen others stratified over it, to the thawing-out of the frozen words as told of by Baron Munchausen and Rabelais, and nobody knows how many others before them.

I was told, within a week, of a business-man in Boston, who, having an important question under consideration, had given it up for the time as too much for him. But he was conscious of an action going on in his brain which was so unusual and painful as to excite his apprehensions that he was threatened with palsy, or something of that sort. After some hours of this uneasiness, his perplexity was

---

[1] Note to "A Voyage to Laputa."

all at once cleared up by the natural solution of his doubt coming to him, — worked out, as he believed, in that obscure and troubled interval.

The cases are numerous where questions have been answered, or problems solved, in dreams, or during unconscious sleep. Two of our most distinguished professors in this institution have had such an experience, as they tell me; and one of them has often assured me that he never dreams. Somnambulism and double-consciousness offer another series of illustrations. Many of my audience remember a murder-case, where the accused was successfully defended, on the ground of somnambulism, by one of the most brilliant of American lawyers. In the year 1686, a brother of Lord Culpeper was indicted at the Old Bailey for shooting one of the guards, and acquitted on the same ground of somnambulism; that is, an unconscious, and therefore irresponsible, state of activity.[1]

---

[1] DALLAS: *The Gay Science*, i. 324.

A more familiar instance of unconscious action is to be found in what we call "absent" persons, — those who, while wide awake, act with an apparent purpose, but without really knowing what they are doing; as in La Bruyère's character, who threw his glass of wine into the backgammon-board, and swallowed the dice.

There are a vast number of movements which we perform with perfect regularity while we are thinking of something quite different, — "automatic actions of the secondary kind," as Hartley calls them, and of which he gives various examples. The old woman knits; the young woman stitches, or perhaps plays her piano, and yet talks away as if nothing but her tongue was busy. Two lovers stroll along side by side, just born into the rosy morning of their new life, prattling the sweet follies worth all the wisdom that years will ever bring them. How much do they think about that wonderful problem of balanced progression which they solve anew at every step?

We are constantly finding results of unperceived mental processes in our consciousness. Here is a striking instance, which I borrow from a recent number of an English journal. It relates to what is considered the most interesting period of incubation in Sir William Rowan Hamilton's discovery of quaternions. The time was the 15th of October, 1843. On that day, he says in a letter to a friend, he was walking from his observatory to Dublin with Lady Hamilton, when, on reaching Brougham Bridge, he "felt the galvanic circle of thought close ; and the sparks that fell from it were the fundamental relations between i, j, k," just as he used them ever afterwards.[1]

Still another instance of the spontaneous evolution of thought we may find in the experience of a great poet. When Goethe shut his eyes, and pictured a flower to himself, he says that it developed itself before him in

---

[1] Nature, Feb. 7, 1870, p. 407 ; North British Review, September, 1866, p. 57.

leaves and blossoms.[1] The result of the mental process appeared as pictured thought, but the process itself was automatic and imperceptible.

There are thoughts that never emerge into consciousness, which yet make their influence felt among the perceptible mental currents, just as the unseen planets sway the movements of those which are watched and mapped by the astronomer. Old prejudices, that are ashamed to confess themselves, nudge our talking thought to utter their magisterial veto. In hours of languor, as Mr. Lecky has remarked, the beliefs and fancies of obsolete conditions are apt to take advantage of us.[2] We know very little of the contents of our minds until some sudden jar brings them to light, as an earthquake that shakes down a miser's house brings out the old stockings full of gold, and all the hoards that have hid away in holes and crannies.

---

[1] Müller's Physiology (Baly's translation), vol ii. p. 1364.

[2] History of Rationalism, ii. 96, *note.*

We not rarely find our personality doubled in our dreams, and do battle with ourselves, unconscious that we are our own antagonists. Dr. Johnson dreamed that he had a contest of wit with an opponent, and got the worst of it: of course, he furnished the wit for both. Tartini heard the Devil play a wonderful sonata, and set it down on awaking. Who was the Devil but Tartini himself? I remember, in my youth, reading verses in a dream, written, as I thought, by a rival fledgling of the Muse. They were so far beyond my powers, that I despaired of equalling them; yet I must have made them unconsciously as I read them. Could I only have remembered them waking!

But I must here add another personal experience, of which I will say beforehand, — somewhat as honest Izaak Walton said of his pike, " This dish of meat is too good for any but anglers or very honest men," — this story is good only for philosophers and very small children. I will merely hint to the former class of thinkers, that its moral bears on two points: first, the value of our self-estimate, sleeping, — possibly, also, waking; secondly, the significance of general formulæ when looked at in certain exalted mental conditions.

I once inhaled a pretty full dose of ether, with the determination to put on record, at the earliest moment of regaining consciousness, the thought I should find uppermost in my mind. The mighty music of the triumphal march into nothingness reverberated through my brain, and filled me with a sense of infinite possibilities, which made me an archangel for the moment. The veil of eternity was lifted. The one great truth which underlies all human experience, and is the key to all the mysteries that philosophy has sought in vain to solve, flashed upon me in a sudden revelation. Henceforth all was clear: a few words had lifted my intelligence to the level of the knowledge of the cherubim. As my natural condition returned, I remembered my resolution; and, staggering to my desk, I wrote, in ill-shaped, straggling characters, the all-embracing truth still glimmering in my consciousness. The words were these (children may smile; the wise will ponder): "*A strong smell of turpentine prevails throughout.*"[1]

My digression has served at least to illustrate the radical change which a slight material cause may produce in our thoughts, and the way we think about them. If the state just described were prolonged, it would be called insanity.[2] I have no doubt that there

---

[1] Sir Humphry Davy has related an experience, which I had forgotten when I recorded my own. After inhaling nitrous-oxide gas, he says, "With the most intense belief and prophetic manner, I exclaimed to Dr. Kingslake, 'Nothing exists but thoughts. The universe is composed of impressions, ideas, pleasures, and pains.'"— *Works*, London, 1839, vol. iii. p. 290.

[2] We are often insane at the moment of awaking from sleep. "'I have desired Apronia to be always careful, especially about the legs.' Pray, do you see any such great wit in that sentence? I must freely own that I do not. Pray, read it over again, and consider it. Why — ay — you must

are many ill-organized, perhaps over-organized, human brains, to which the common air is what the vapor of ether was to mine : it is madness to them to drink in this terrible burning oxygen at every breath ; and the atmosphere that infolds them is like the flaming shirt of Nessus.

The more we examine the mechanism of thought, the more we shall see that the automatic, unconscious action of the mind enters largely into all its processes. Our definite

---

know that I dreamed it just now, and waked with it in my mouth. Are you bit, or are you not, sirrahs ? " — SWIFT's *Journal to Stella*, Letter xv.

Even when wide awake, so keen and robust a mind as Swift's was capable of a strange momentary aberration in the days of its full vigor. "I have my mouth full of water, and was going to spit it out, because I reasoned with myself, 'How could I write when my mouth was full?' Have you not done things like that, — reasoned wrong at first thinking?" — *Ibid.*, Letter viii.

All of us must have had similar experiences.

ideas are stepping-stones ; how we get from one to the other, we do not know : something carries us ; we do not take the step. A creating and informing spirit which is with us, and not of us, is recognized everywhere in real and in storied life. It is the Zeus that kindled the rage of Achilles ; it is the Muse of Homer ; it is the Daimon of Socrates ; it is the inspiration of the seer ; it is the mocking devil that whispers to Margaret as she kneels at the altar ; and the hobgoblin that cried, "Sell him, sell him!" in the ear of John Bunyan : it shaped the forms that filled the soul of Michael Angelo when he saw the figure of the great Lawgiver in the yet unhewn marble, and the dome of the world's yet unbuilt basilica against the blank horizon ; it comes to the least of us, as a voice that will be heard ; it tells us what we must believe ; it frames our sentences ; it lends a sudden gleam of sense or eloquence to the dullest of us all, so that, like Katterfelto with his hair on end, we wonder at ourselves, or rather not at ourselves, but at this divine

4

visitor, who chooses our brain as his dwell
ing-place, and invests our naked thought
with the purple of the kings of speech or
song.

After all, the mystery of unconscious
mental action is exemplified, as I have said,
in every act of mental association. What
happens when one idea brings up another?
Some internal movement, of which we are
wholly unconscious, and which we only
know by its effect. What is this action,
which in Dame Quickly agglutinates contigu-
ous circumstances by their surfaces; in men
of wit and fancy, connects remote ideas by
partial resemblances; in men of imagination,
by the vital identity which underlies phenom-
enal diversity; in the man of science, groups
the objects of thought in sequences of maximum resemblance? Not one of them can
answer. There is a Delphi and a Pythoness
in every human breast.

The poet sits down to his desk with an odd
conceit in his brain; and presently his eyes
fill with tears, his thought slides into the

minor key, and his heart is full of sad and plaintive melodies. Or he goes to his work, saying, "To-night I would have tears;" and, before he rises from his table, he has written a burlesque, such as he might think fit to send to one of the comic papers, if these were not so commonly cemeteries of hilarity interspersed with cenotaphs of wit and humor. These strange hysterics of the intelligence, which make us pass from weeping to laughter, and from laughter back again to weeping, must be familiar to every impressible nature; and all is as automatic, involuntary, as entirely self-evolved by a hidden organic process, as are the changing moods of the laughing and crying woman. The poet always recognizes a dictation *ab extra;* and we hardly think it a figure of speech when we talk of his inspiration.

The mental attitude of the poet while writing, if I may venture to define it, is that of the " nun, breathless with adoration." Mental stillness is the first condition of the listen-

ing state ; and I think my friends the poets
will recognize that the sense of effort, which
is often felt, accompanies the mental spasm
by which the mind is maintained in a state at
once passive to the influx from without, and
active in seizing only that which will serve
its purpose.[1] It is not strange that remem-

---

[1] Burns tells us how he composed verses for a
given tune : —

"My way is, I consider the poetic sentiment
correspondent to my idea of the musical expression; then choose my theme; begin one stanza.
When that is composed, which is generally the
most difficult part of the business, I walk out, sit
down now and then, look out for objects in Nature
that are in unison or harmony with the cogitations
of my fancy, and workings of my bosom; hum-
ming every now and then the air with the verses
I have framed. When I feel my Muse beginning
to jade, I retire to the solitary fireside of my
study, and there commit my effusions to paper;
swinging at intervals on the hind-legs of my
elbow-chair, by way of calling forth my own critical strictures, as my pen goes on." — *Letters to G.
Thomson*, No. xxxvii.

bered ideas should often take advantage of the crowd of thoughts, and smuggle themselves in as original. Honest thinkers are always stealing unconsciously from each other. Our minds are full of waifs and estrays which we think are our own. Innocent plagiarism turns up everywhere. Our best musical critic tells me that a few notes of the air of " Shoo Fly " are borrowed from a movement in one of the magnificent harmonies of Beethoven.[1]

---

[1] One or two instances where the same idea is found in different authors may be worth mentioning in illustration of the remark just made. We are familiar with the saying, that the latest days are the old age of the world.

Mr. Lewes finds this in Lord Bacon's writings, in Roger Bacon's also, and traces it back as far as Seneca. I find it in Pascal (*Préface sur le Traité du Vide*); and Hobbes says, " If we will reverence the ages, the present is the oldest." So, too, Tennyson : —

> " For we are ancients of the earth,
> And in the morning of the times."
>
> *The Day-Dream: L'Envoi*

And so the orator, — I do not mean the poor slave of a manuscript, who takes his thought chilled and stiffened from its mould, but the impassioned speaker who pours it

---

Here are several forms of another familiar thought : —

> " And what if all of animated nature
> Be but organic harps diversely framed,
> That tremble into thought as o'er them sweeps,
> Plastic and vast, one intellectual breeze,
> At once the soul of each, and God of all ? "
>
> COLERIDGE : *The Æolian Harp.*

" Are we a piece of machinery, which, like the Æolian harp, passive, takes the impression of the passing accident ? " — BURNS TO MRS. DUNLOP : *Letter* 148.

" Un seul esprit, qui est universel et qui anime tout l'univers, — comme un même souffle de vent fait sonner differemment divers tuyaux d'orgue." — LEIBNITZ : *Considérations sur la Doctrine d'un Esprit Universel.*

Literature is full of such coincidences, which some love to believe plagiarisms. There are thoughts always abroad in the air, which it takes more wit to avoid than to hit upon, as the solitary " Address without a Phœnix " may remind those

forth as it flows coruscating from the furnace, — the orator only becomes our master at the moment when he himself is surprised, captured, taken possession of, by a sudden rush of fresh inspiration. How well

---

critical ant-eaters whose aggressive feature is drawn to too fine a point.

Old stories reproduce themselves in a singular way, — not only in such authors as Mr. Joseph Miller, but among those whom we cannot for a moment suspect of conscious misappropriation. Here is an instance forced upon my attention. In the preface to "The Guardian Angel," I quoted a story from Sprague's "Annals of the American Pulpit," which is there spoken of as being told, by Jonathan Edwards the younger, of a brutal fellow in New Haven. Some one found a similar story in a German novel, and mentioned the coincidence. The true original, to which I was directed by Dr. Elam's book, "A Physician's Problems," is to be found in the seventh chapter of the seventh book of Aristotle's Ethics. My Latin version renders it thus: "Et qui a filio trahebatur trahendi finem jubebat ad fores, nam a se quoque ad hunc locum patrem suum tractum esse."

we know the flash of the eye, the thrill of the voice, which are the signature and symbol of nascent thought, — thought just emerging into consciousness, in which condition, as is the case with the chemist's elements, it has a combining force at other times wholly unknown!

But we are all more or less improvisators. We all have a double, who is wiser and better than we are, and who puts thoughts into our heads, and words into our mouths. Do we not all commune with our own hearts upon our beds? Do we not all divide ourselves, and go to buffets on questions of right or wrong, of wisdom or folly? Who or what is it that resolves the stately parliament of the day, with all its forms and conventionalities and pretences, and the great Me presiding, into the committee of the whole, with Conscience in the chair, that holds its solemn session through the watches of the night?

Persons who talk most do not always think most. I question whether persons who think most — that is, have most conscious thought

pass through their minds — necessarily do
most mental work. The tree you are stick-
ing in " will be growing when you are sleeping." So with every new idea that is planted
in a real thinker's mind : it will be growing
when he is least conscious of it. An idea in
the brain is not a legend carved on a marble
slab : it is an impression made on a living
tissue, which is the seat of active nutritive
processes. Shall the initials I carved in bark
increase from year to year with the tree ? and
shall not my recorded thought develop into
new forms and relations with my growing
brain ? Mr. Webster told one of our greatest
scholars that he had to change the size of
his hat every few years. His head grew
larger as his intellect expanded. Illustrations of this same fact were shown me many
years ago by Mr. Deville, the famous phre-
nologist, in London. But organic mental
changes may take place in shorter spaces of
time. A single night of sleep has often
brought a sober second-thought, which was a
surprise to the hasty conclusion of the day

before. Lord Polkommet's description of the way he prepared himself for a judicial decision is in point, except for the alcoholic fertilizer he employed in planting his ideas: " Ye see, I first read a' the pleadings; and then, after letting them wamble in my wame wi' the toddy two or three days, I gie my ain interlocutor." [1]

The counterpart of this slow process is found in the ready, spontaneous, automatic, self-sustaining, continuous flow of thought, well illustrated in a certain form of dialogue, which seems to be in a measure peculiar to the female sex. The sternest of our sisters will, I hope, forgive me for telling the way in which this curious fact was forced upon my notice.

I was passing through a somewhat obscure street at the west end of our city a year or two since, when my attention was attracted to a narrow court by a sound of voices and a

---

[1] Dean Ramsay's Reminiscences of Scottish Life and Character, p. 126.

small crowd of listeners. From two open
windows on the opposite sides of the court
projected the heads, and a considerable portion of the persons, of two of the sex in
question, — natives, both of them, apparently,
of the green isle famous for shamrocks and
shillalahs. They were engaged in argument,
if that is argument in which each of the
two parties develops his proposition without
the least regard to what the other is at the
same time saying. The question involved
was the personal, social, moral, and, in short,
total standing and merit of the two contro-
versialists and their respective families. But
the strange phenomenon was this : The
two women, as if by preconcerted agreement,
like two instruments playing a tune in
unison, were pouring forth simultaneously
a calm, steady, smooth-flowing stream of
mutual undervaluation, to apply a mild
phrase to it ; never stopping for punctuation,
and barely giving themselves time to get
breath between its long-drawn clauses. The
dialogue included every conceivable taunt

which might rouse the fury of a sensitive mother of a family, whose allegiance to her lord, and pride in her offspring, were points which it displeased her to have lightly handled. I stood and listened like the quiet groups in the more immediate neighborhood. I looked for some explosion of violence, for a screaming volley of oaths, for an hysteric burst of tears, perhaps for a missile of more questionable character than an epithet aimed at the head and shoulders projecting opposite. " At any rate," I thought, " their tongues will soon run down ; for it is not in human nature that such a flow of scalding rhetoric can be kept up very long." But I stood waiting until I was tired ; and, with *labitur et labetur* on my lips, I left them pursuing the even tenor, or treble, of their way in a duet which seemed as if it might go on until nightfall.

I came away thinking I had discovered a new national custom, as peculiar, and probably as limited, as the Corsican vendetta. But I have since found that the same scolding duets take place between the women in an African kraal. A couple of them will thrust their bodies half out of their huts, and exhaust the vocabulary of the native Worcester and Webster to each other's detriment, while the bystanders listen with a sympathy which often leads to a general disturbance.[1] And I find that Homer was before us all in noticing this curious logomachy of the unwarlike sex. Æneas says to Achilles after an immensely long-winded discourse, which Creüsa could hardly have outdone, —

> " But why in wordy and contentious strife
> Need we each other scold, as women use,
> Who, with some heart-consuming anger wroth,
> Stand in the street, and call each other names,
> Some true, some false ; for so their rage commands ? ' [2]

---

[1] Uncivilized Races of Men. By Rev. J. G. Wood. Vol. i. p. 213.

[2] *Iliad,* xx. 251–255. And Tennyson speaks of

> " Those detestable
> That let the bantling scald at home, and brawl
> Their rights or wrongs like pot-herbs in the street."
>
> *The Princess,* 323.

I confess that the recollection of the two
women, drifting upon their vocabularies as
on a shoreless ocean, filled me at first with
apprehension as to the possible future of our
legislative assemblies. But, in view of what
our own sex accomplishes in the line of
mutual vituperation, perhaps the feminine
arrangement, by which the two save time
by speaking at once, and it is alike impossible
for either to hear the other, and for the audience to hear them both, might be considered
an improvement.

The automatic flow of thought is often
singularly favored by the fact of listening
to a weak, continuous discourse, with just
enough ideas in it to keep the mind busy on
something else. The *induced current* of
thought is often rapid and brilliant in the
inverse ratio of the force of the inducing current.

The vast amount of blood sent to the
brain implies a corresponding amount of
material activity in the organ. In point of
fact, numerous experiments have shown (and

I may refer particularly to those of our own countrymen, — Professors Flint, Hammond, and Lombard) that the brain is the seat of constant nutritive changes, which are greatly increased by mental exertion.

The mechanical co-efficient of mental action may be therefore considered a molecular movement in the nervous centres, attended with waste of material conveyed thither in the form of blood, — not a mere tremor like the quiver of a bell, but a process more like combustion ; the blood carrying off the oxidated particles, and bringing in fresh matter to take their place.

This part of the complex process must, of course, enter into the category of the correlated forces. The brain must be fed in order to work ; and according to the amount of waste of material will be that of the food required to repair losses. So much logic, so much beef; so much poetry, so much pudding : and, as we all know that all growing things are but sponges soaked full of old sunshine, Apollo becomes as important in the world of letters as ever.[1]

But the intellectual product does not belong to the category of force at all, as defined by physicists. It does not answer their definition as "that which is expended in producing or resisting motion." It is not reconvertible into other forms of force. One cannot lift a weight with a logical demonstration, or make a tea-kettle boil by writing an ode to it. A given amount of molecular action in two brains represents a certain equivalent of food, but by no means an equivalent of intellectual product. Bavius and Mævius were very probably as good feeders as Virgil and Horace, and wasted as much brain-tissue in producing their *carmina* as the two great masters wasted in producing theirs. It may be doubted whether the present Laureate of England consumed more

---

[1] It is curious to compare the Laputan idea of extracting sunbeams from cucumbers with George Stephenson's famous saying about coal.

oxidable material in the shape of nourishment for every page of "Maud" or of "In Memoriam" than his predecessor Nahum Tate, whose masterpiece gets no better eulogy than that it is "the least miserable of his productions," in eliminating an equal amount of verse.[1]

As mental labor, in distinction from the passive flow of thought, implies an exercise of will, and as mental labor is shown to be attended by an increased waste, the pre-

---

[1] "Sur un même papier, avec la même plume et la même encre, en remuant tant soit peu le bout de la plume en certaine façon, vous tracez des lettres qui font imaginer des combats, des tempêtes ou des furies à ceux qui les lisent, et qui les rendent indignés ou tristes; au lieu que si vous remuez la plume d'une autre façon presque semblable, la seule différence qui sera en ce peu de mouvement leur peut donner des pensées toutes contraires, comme de paix, de repos, de douceur, et exciter en eux des passions d'amour et de joie."—DESCARTES: *Principes de Philosophie*, 4ème Partie, § 197.

sumption is that this waste is in some degree referable to the material requirements of the act of volition. We see why the latter should be attended by a sense of effort, and followed by a feeling of fatigue.

A question is suggested by the definition of the physicists. What is that which changes the form of force ? Electricity leaves what we call magnetism in iron, after passing through it: what name shall we give to that virtue in iron which causes the force we know as electricity thus to manifest itself by a precipitate, so to speak, of new properties? Why may we not speak of a *vis ferrea* as causing the change in consequence of which a bar through which an electrical current has flowed becomes capable of attracting iron and of magnetizing a million other bars? And so why may not a particular brain, through which certain nutritious currents have flowed, fix a force derived from these currents in virtue of a *vis Platonica* or a *vis Baconica*, and thus become a magnet in the universe of thought, exercising and imparting an influence which is not expended, in addition to that accounted for by the series of molecular changes in the thinking organ ?

We must not forget that force-equivalent is one thing, and quality of force-product is quite a different thing. The same outlay of muscular exertion turns the winch of a coffee-mill and of a hand-organ. It has been said that thought cannot be a physical force, because it cannot be measured. An attempt has been made to measure thought as we measure force. I have two tables, one from the "Annales Encyclopédiques," and another, earlier and less minute, by the poet Akenside, in which the poets are classified according to their distinctive qualities; each quality and the total average being marked on a scale of twenty as a maximum. I am not sure that mental qualities are not as susceptible of measurement as the aurora borealis or the changes of the weather. But even measurable *quality* has no more to do with the correlation of forces than the color of a horse with his power of draught; and it is with quality we more especially deal in intellect and morals.

I have spoken of the material or physiological co-efficient of thought as being indispensable for its exercise during the only condition of existence of which, apart from any alleged spiritualistic experience, we have any personal knowledge. We know our dependence too well from seeing so many gallant and well-freighted minds towed in helpless after a certain time of service, — razees at sixty, dismantled at seventy, going to pieces and sinking at fourscore. We recognize in ourselves the loss of mental power, slight or serious, from grave or trifling causes. "Good God," said Swift, "what a genius I had when I wrote that book!" And I remember that an ingenious tailor of the neighboring city, on seeing a customer leave his shop without purchasing, exclaimed, smiting his forehead, "If it had not been for this — emphatically characterized — headache, I'd have had a coat on that man before he'd got out over my doorstep."

Such is the delicate adjustment of the intellectual apparatus by the aid of which we clothe our neighbor, whether he will or no, with our thoughts if we are writers of books, with our garments if we are artificers of habiliments.

The problem of memory is closely connected with the question of the mechanical relation between thought and structure. How intimate is the alliance of memory with the material condition of the brain, is shown by the effect of age, of disease, of a blow, of intoxication. I have known an aged person repeat the same question five, six, or seven times during the same brief visit. Everybody knows the archbishop's flavor of apoplexy in the memory as in the other mental powers. I was once asked to see to a woman who had just been injured in the street. On coming to herself, " Where am I? what has happened ? " she asked. " Knocked down by a horse, ma'am ; stunned a little : that is all." A pause, " while one with moderate haste might count a hundred ; "

and then again, " Where am I ? what has happened ? " — " Knocked down by a horse, ma'am ; stunned a little : that is all." Another pause, and the same question again ; and so on during the whole time I was by her. The same tendency to repeat a question indefinitely has been observed in returning members of those worshipping assemblies whose favorite hymn is, " We won't go home till morning."

Is memory, then, a material record ? Is the brain, like the rocks of the Sinaitic Valley, written all over with inscriptions left by the long caravans of thought, as they have passed year after year through its mysterious recesses ?

When we see a distant railway-train sliding by us in the same line, day after day, we infer the existence of a track which guides it. So, when some dear old friend begins that story we remember so well ; switching off at the accustomed point of digression ; coming to a dead stop at the puzzling question of chronology ; off the track on the

matter of its being first or second cousin of
somebody's aunt; set on it again by the
patient, listening wife, who knows it all as she
knows her well-worn wedding-ring, — how
can we doubt that there is a track laid down
for the story in some permanent disposition
of the thinking-marrow ?

I need not say that no microscope can find
the tablet inscribed with the names of early
loves, the stains left by tears of sorrow or
contrition, the rent where the thunderbolt of
passion has fallen, or any legible token that
such experiences have formed a part of the
life of the mortal, the vacant temple of whose
thought it is exploring. It is only as an
inference, aided by an illustration which I
will presently offer, that I suggest the possible existence, in the very substance of the
brain-tissue, of those inscriptions which
Shakspeare must have thought of when he
wrote, —

> " Pluck from the memory a rooted sorrow ;
> Raze out the written troubles of the brain."

The objection to the existence of such a

material record — that we renew our bodies many scores of times, and yet retain our earliest recollections — is entirely met by the fact, that a scar of any kind holds its own pretty nearly through life in spite of all these same changes, as we have not far to look to find instances.

It must be remembered that a billion of the starry brain-cells could be packed in a cubic inch, and that the convolutions contain one hundred and thirty-four cubic inches, according to the estimate already given. My illustration is derived from microscopic photography. I have a glass slide on which is a minute photographic picture, which is exactly covered when the head of a small pin is laid upon it. In that little speck are clearly to be seen, by a proper magnifying power, the following objects: the Declaration of Independence, with easily-recognized facsimile autographs of all the signers; the arms of all the original thirteen States; the Capitol at Washington; and very good portraits of all the Presidents of the

United States from Washington to Mr. James
K. Polk. These objects are all distinguisha-
ble as a group with a power of fifty diame-
ters: with a power of three hundred, any
one of them becomes a sizable picture. You
may see, if you will, the majesty of Washington on his noble features, or the will of
Jackson in those hard lines of the long face,
crowned with that bristling head of hair in
a perpetual state of electrical divergence
and centrifugal self - assertion. Remember
that each of these faces is the record of a
life.

Now recollect that there was an interval
between the exposure of the negative in the
camera and its development by pouring a
wash over it, when all these pictured objects
existed potentially, but absolutely invisible,
and incapable of recognition, in a speck of col-
lodion-film, which a pin's head would cover,
and then think what Alexandrian libraries,
what Congressional document-loads of posi-
tively intelligible characters, — such as one
look of the recording angel would bring out;

many of which we can ourselves develop
at will, or which come before our eyes unbid-
den, like " Mene, Mene, Tekel, Upharsin,"
— might be held in those convolutions of the
brain which wrap the talent intrusted to us,
too often as the folded napkin of the slothful
servant hid the treasure his master had lent
him ! [1]

---

[1] " Eas mutationes in sensorio conservatas, *ideas*
multi, nos vestigia rerum vocabimus, quæ non in
mente sed in ipso corpore, et in medulla quidem
cerebri ineffabili modo incredibiliter *minutis notis*
et copia infinita inscriptæ sunt." — HALLER, quoted by Dr. LAYCOCK : *Brit. and For. Med. Rev.*, xix.
310.

"Different matters are arranged in my head,"
said Napoleon, "as in drawers.   I open one drawer,
and close another, as I wish.   I have never been
kept awake by an involuntary pre-occupation of
the mind.   If I desire repose, I shut up all the
drawers, and sleep.   I have always slept when I
wanted rest, and almost at will." — *Table-Talk and
Opinions of Napoleon Buonaparte*, London, 1869,
p. 10.

Three facts, so familiar that I need only allude to them, show how much more is recorded in the memory than we may ever take cognizance of. The first is the conviction of having been in the same precise circumstances once or many times before. Dr. Wigan says, never but once; but such is not my experience. The second is the panorama of their past lives, said, by people rescued from drowning, to have flashed before them.[1]

---

[1] The following story is related as fact. I condense it from the newspaper account.

"A held a bond against B for several hundred dollars. When it became due, he searched for it, but could not find it. He told the facts to B, who denied having given the bond, and intimated a fraudulent design on the part of A, who was compelled to submit to his loss and the charge against him. Years afterward, A was bathing in Charles River, when he was seized with cramp, and nearly drowned. On coming to his senses, he went to his bookcase, took out a book, and from between its leaves took the missing bond. In the sudden picture of his entire life, which flashed before him

I had it once myself, accompanied by an ignoble ducking and scrambling self-rescue. The third is the revival of apparently obsolete impressions, of which many strange cases are related in nervous young women and in dying persons, and which the story of the dog Argus in the "Odyssey," and of the parrot so charmingly told by Campbell, would lead us to suppose not of rare occurrence in animals.[1] It is possible, therefore,

---

as he was sinking, the act of putting the bond in the book, and the book in the bookcase, had represented itself."

The reader who likes to hear the whole of a story may be pleased to learn that the debt was paid *with interest.*

[1] "A troop of cavalry which had served on the Continent was disbanded in York. Sir Robert Clayton turned out the old horses in Knavesmire to have their run for life. One day, while grazing promiscuously and apart from each other, a storm gathered; and, when the thunder pealed and the lightning flashed, they were seen to get together, and form in line, in almost as perfect order as

and I have tried to show that it is not im-
probable, that memory is a material record;
that the brain is scarred and seamed with
infinitesimal hieroglyphics, as the features
are engraved with the traces of thought and
passion. And, if this is so, must not the
record, we ask, perish with the organ? Alas!
how often do we see it perish *before* the
organ! — the mighty satirist tamed into obliv-
ious imbecility; the great scholar wandering
without sense of time or place among his
alcoves, taking his books one by one from the
shelves, and fondly patting them; a child

---

if they had had their old masters on their backs." —
LAYCOCK : *Brit. and For. Med. Rev.*, vol. xix. 309.

" After the slaughter at Vionville, on the 18th
of August (last), a strange and touching specta-
cle was presented. On the evening-call being
sounded by the first regiment of Dragoons of the
Guard, six hundred and two riderless horses answered to the summons, —jaded, and in many
cases maimed. The noble animals still retained
their disciplined habits." — *German Post*, quoted
by the *Spectator*.

once more among his toys, but a child whose
to-morrows come hungry, and not full-handed,
— come as birds of prey in the place of the
sweet singers of morning. We must all become as little children if we live long enough;
but how blank an existence the wrinkled in-
fant must carry into the kingdom of heaven,
if the Power that gave him memory does not
repeat the miracle by restoring it !

The connection between thought and the
structure and condition of the brain is evi-
dently so close, that all we have to do is to
study it. It is not in this direction that
materialism is to be feared : we do not find
Hamlet and Faust, right and wrong, the
valor of men and the purity of women, by
testing for albumen, or examining fibres in
microscopes.

It is in the moral world that materialism
has worked the strangest confusion. In various forms, under imposing names and aspects,
it has thrust itself into the moral relations,
until one hardly knows where to look for any

first principles without upsetting every thing in searching for them.

The moral universe includes nothing but the exercise of choice : all else is machinery. What we can help and what we cannot help are on two sides of a line which separates the sphere of human responsibility from that of the Being who has arranged and controls the order of things.

The question of the freedom of the will has been an open one, from the days of Milton's demons in conclave, to the recent most noteworthy essay of Mr. Hazard, our Rhode-Island neighbor.[1] It still hangs suspended between the seemingly exhaustive strongest motive argument and certain residual convictions. The sense that we are, to a limited extent, self-determining ; the sense of effort in willing ; the sense of responsibility in view of the future, and the verdict of conscience

---

[1] " Witness on him that any parfit clerk is,
    That in scole is gret altercation
    In this matere, and gret disputison,
    And hath ben, of an hundred thousand men ;
    But I ne cannot boult it to the bren."
        CHAUCER : *The Nonne's Preeste's Tale*

in review of the past, — all of these are open
to the accusation of fallacy; but they all leave
a certain undischarged balance in most minds.[1]
We can invoke the strong arm of the *Deus
ex machina*, as Mr. Hazard, and Kant and
others, before him, have done. Our will may
be a primary initiating cause or force, as un-
explainable, as unreducible, as indecomposa-
ble, as impossible if you choose, but as real
to our belief, as the *æternitas a parte ante*.
The divine foreknowledge is no more in the
way of delegated choice than the divine om-
nipotence is in the way of delegated power.
The Infinite can surely slip the cable of the
finite if it choose so to do.

---

[1] " But, sir, as to the doctrine of necessity, no
man believes it. If a man should give me argu-
ments that I do not see, though I could not answer
them, should I believe that I do not see?"—Boswell's *Life of Johnson*. London, 1848, vol. viii.
p. 331.

" What have you to do with liberty and necessity? or what more than to hold your tongue
about it ? " — JOHNSON TO BOSWELL : *Ibid.*,
Letter 396.

It is one thing to prove a proposition like the doctrine of necessity in terms, and another thing to accept it as an article of faith. There are cases in which I would oppose to the *credo quia impossibile est* a paradox as bold and as serviceable, — *nego quia probatum est.* Even Mr. Huxley, who throws quite as much responsibility on protoplasm as it will bear, allows that "our volition counts for something as a condition of the course of events."

I reject, therefore, the mechanical doctrine which makes me the slave of outside influences, whether it work with the logic of Edwards, or the averages of Buckle; whether it come in the shape of the Greek's destiny, or the Mahometan's fatalism; or in that other aspect, dear to the band of believers, whom Beesly of Everton, speaking in the character of John Wesley, characterized as

"The crocodile crew that believe in election." [1]

---

[1] SOUTHEY's *Life of Wesley*, vol. ii. note 28.

But I claim the right to eliminate all mechanical ideas which have crowded into the sphere of intelligent choice between right and wrong. The pound of flesh I will grant to Nemesis; but, in the name of human nature, not one drop of blood, — not one drop.

Moral chaos began with the idea of transmissible responsibility.[1] It seems the stalest

---

[1] "Il est sans doute qu'il n'y-a rien qui choque plus notre raison que de dire que le péché du premier homme ait rendu coupables ceux qui, étant si éloignés de cette source, semblent incapables d'y participer. Cet écoulement ne nous parait pas seulement impossible, il nous semble même très injuste; car qu'y-a-t-il de plus contraire au règles de notre misérable justice que de damner éternellement un enfant incapable de volonté, pour un péché où il paraît avoir si peu de part, qu'il est commis six mille ans avant qu'il fût en être?"— PASCAL: *Pensées*, c. x. § I.

"Justice" and "Mercy" often have a technical meaning when applied to the Supreme Being. Mr. J. S. Mill has expressed himself very freely

of truisms to say that every moral act, depending as it does on choice, is in its nature exclusively personal ; that its penalty, if it have any, is payable, not to bearer, not to order, but only to the creditor himself. To treat

---

as to this juggling with words. — *Examination of Sir W. Hamilton's Philosophy,* i. 131.

The Romanists fear for the future welfare of babes that perish unborn ; and the extraordinary means that are taken to avert their impending "punishment" are well known.

Thomas Shepard, our famous Cambridge minister, seems to have shared these apprehensions. — *See his Letter in Young's Chronicles of the Pilgrims of Massachusetts,* p. 538. Boston, 1846.

The author of " The Day of Doom " is forced by his logic to hand the infants over to the official tormentor, only assigning them the least uncomfortable of the torture-chambers.

However these doctrines may be softened in the belief of many, the primary barbarism on which they rest — that is, the transfer of mechanical ideas into the world of morals, with which they are in no sense homologous — is almost universally prevalent, and like to be at present.

a mal-volition, which is inseparably involved with an internal condition, as capable of external transfer from one person to another, is simply to materialize it. When we can take the dimensions of virtue by triangulation; when we can literally weigh Justice in her own scales; when we can speak of the specific gravity of truth, or the square root of honesty; when we can send a statesman his integrity in a package to Washington, if he happen to have left it behind, — then we may begin to speak of the moral character of inherited tendencies, which belong to the machinery for which the Sovereign Power alone is responsible. The misfortune of perverse instincts, which adhere to us as congenital inheritances, should go to our side of the account, if the books of heaven are kept, as the great Church of Christendom maintains they are, by double entry. But the absurdity which has been held up to ridicule in the nursery has been enforced as the highest reason upon older children. Did our forefathers tolerate Æsop among them? "I cannot trouble the water where you are," says the lamb to the wolf: "don't you see that I am farther down the stream?"—"But a year ago you called me ill names."—"O sir! a year ago I was not born."—"Sirrah," replies the wolf, "if it was not you, it was your father, and that is all one;" and finishes with the usual practical application.

If a created being has no rights which his Creator is bound to respect, there is an end to all moral relations between them. Good Father Abraham thought he had, and did not hesitate to give his opinion. "Far be it from Thee," he says, to do so and so. And Pascal, whose reverence amounted to theophobia,[1] could treat of the duties of the Su-

---

[1] I use this term to designate a state of mind thus described by Jeremy Taylor: "There are some persons so miserable and scrupulous, such perpetual tormentors of themselves with unnecessary fears, that their meat and drink is a snare to their consciences.

"These persons do not believe noble things of God."

preme to the dependent being.[1]   If we suffer
for any thing except our own wrong-doing,
to call it punishment is like speaking of a
yard of veracity or a square inch of magna-
nimity.

So to rate the gravity of a mal-volition by
its consequences is the merest sensational materialism.   A little child takes a prohibited
friction-match : it kindles a conflagration with
it, which burns down the house, and perishes
itself in the flames.   Mechanically, this child
was an incendiary and a suicide; morally,
neither.   Shall we hesitate to speak as chari-
tably of multitudes of weak and ignorant
grown-up children, moving about on a planet
whose air is a deadly poison, which kills all
that breathe it four or five scores of years ?

Closely allied to this is the pretence that
the liabilities incurred by any act of mal-voli-

---

[1] "Il y a un devoir réciproque entre Dieu et les
hommes. . . . *Quid debui?* 'accusez moi,' dit Dieu
dans Isaïe.   Dieu doit accomplir ses promesses,"
&c. — *Pensées,* xxiii. 3.

tion are to be measured on the scale of the
Infinite, and not on that of the total moral
capacity of the finite agent, — a mechanical
application of the Oriental way of dealing
with offences. The sheik or sultan chops a
man's head off for a look he does not like: it
is not the amount of wrong, but the importance of the personage who has been out-
raged. We have none of those moral relations with power, as such, which the habitual
Eastern modes of speech seem to imply.

The next movement in moral materialism
is to establish a kind of scale of equivalents
between perverse moral choice and physical
suffering. Pain often cures *ignorance*, as we
know, — as when a child learns not to handle
fire by burning its fingers, — but it does not
change the moral nature.[1] Children may
be whipped into obedience, but not into virtue; and it is not pretended that the penal

---

[1] "No troubles will, of themselves, work a
change in a wicked heart." — MATTHEW HENRY:
Com. on Luke, xxiii. 29.

colony of heaven has sent back a single re-
formed criminal. We hang men for our con-
venience or safety; sometimes shoot them for
revenge. Thus we come to associate the in-
fliction of injury with offences as their satis-
factory settlement, — a kind of neutralization
of them, as of an acid with an alkali: so that
we feel as if a jarring moral universe would be
all right if only suffering enough were added
to it. This scheme of chemical equivalents
seems to me, I confess, a worse materialism
than making protoplasm master of arts, and
doctor of divinity.

Another mechanical notion is that which
treats moral evil as bodily disease has so long
been treated, — as being a distinct entity, a
demon to be expelled, a load to be got rid
of, instead of a condition, or the result of a
condition.[1] But what is most singular in the
case of moral disease is, that it has been forgotten that it is a living creature in which it

---

[1] "The strength of modern therapeutics lies in
the clearer perception, than formerly, of the great

occurs, and that all living creatures are the subjects of natural and spontaneous healing processes. A broken vase cannot mend itself; but a broken bone can. Nature, that is, the Divinity, in his every-day working methods, will soon make it as strong as ever.

Suppose the beneficent self-healing process to have repaired the wound in the moral nature: is it never to become an honest scar, but always liable to be re-opened? Is there no outlawry of an obsolete self-determination? If the President of the Society for the Prevention of Cruelty to Animals impaled a fly on a pin when he was ten years old, is it to stand against him, crying for a stake through his body, *in sæcula sæculorum?* [1] The most popu-

---

truth, that diseases are but perverted life-processes, and have for their natural history, not only a beginning, but equally a period of culmination and decline." — *Medicine in Modern Times.* Dr. GULL's *Address*, p. 187.

[1] There is no more significant evidence of natural moral evolution than the way in which children

lar hymn of Protestantism, and the "Dies Iræ" of Romanism, are based on this assumption : *Nil inultum remanebit.* So it is that a condition of a conscious being has been materialized into a purely inorganic brute fact, — not merely dehumanized, but de-animalized and devitalized.

Here it was that Swedenborg, whose whole secret I will not pretend to have fully opened, though I have tried with the key of a thinker whom I love and honor, — that Swedenborg, I say, seems to have come in, if not with a new revelation, at least infusing new life into the earlier ones. *What we are* will determine the company we are to keep, and not the avoirdupois weight of our moral exuviæ, strapped on our shoulders like a porter's burden.

---

outgrow the cruelty which is so common in what we call their *tender* years.

> " As ruthless as a baby with a worm ;
> As cruel as a schoolboy ere he grows
> To pity, — more from ignorance than will."
>   TENNYSON : *Walking to the Mail.*

Having once materialized the whole province of self-determination and its consequences, the next thing is, of course, to materialize the methods of avoiding these consequences. We are all, more or less, idolaters, and believers in quackery. We love specifics better than regimen, and observances better than self-government. The moment our belief divorces itself from character, the mechanical element begins to gain upon it, and tends to its logical conclusion in the Japanese prayer-mill.[1]

---

[1] One can easily conceive the confusion which might be wrought in young minds by such teaching as this of our excellent Thomas Shepard: —

" The Paths to Hell be but two : the first is the Path of Sin, which is a dirty Way; Secondly, the Path of Duties, which (rested in) is but a cleaner Way." — Quoted by Israel Loring, Pastor of the West Church in Sudbury, in " *A Practical Discourse,*" &c. Boston : Kneeland and Green, 1749.

However sound the doctrine, it is sure to lead to the substitution of some easy mechanical contri-

Brothers of the Phi Beta Kappa Society, my slight task is finished. I have always regarded these occasions as giving an opportunity of furnishing hints for future study, rather than of exhibiting the detailed results of thought. I cannot but hope that I have thrown some ray of suggestion, or brought out some clink of questionable soundness, which will justify me for appearing with the lantern and the hammer.

The hardest and most painful task of the student of to-day is to occidentalize and modernize the Asiatic modes of thought which have come down to us closely wedded to mediæval interpretations. We are called upon to assert the rights and dignity of our humanity, if it were only that our worship might be worthy the acceptance of a wise and magnanimous Sovereign. Self-abasement is the proper sign of homage to superiors with

---

vance — some rite, penance, or formula — for perpetual and ever-renewed acts of moral self-determination.

the Oriental. The Occidental demands self-respect in his inferiors as a condition of accepting their tribute to him as of any value. The *kotou* in all its forms, the pitiful acts of *creeping, crawling, fawning, like a dog at his master's feet*, (which acts are signified by the word we translate *worship*, according to the learned editor of " The Comprehensive Commentary,")[1] are offensive, not gratifying, to him. Does not the man of science who accepts with true manly reverence the facts of Nature, in the face of all his venerated traditions, offer a more acceptable service than he who repeats the formulæ, and copies the gestures, derived from the language and customs of despots and their subjects? The attitude of modern Science is erect, her aspect serene, her determination inexorable, her onward movement unflinching ; because she believes herself, in the order of Providence, the true successor of the men of old who brought down the light of heaven to men. She has

---

[1] See note on Matthew, xi. 11.

reclaimed astronomy and cosmogony, and is already laying a firm hand on anthropology, over which another battle must be fought, with the usual result, to come sooner or later. Humility may be taken for granted as existing in every sane human being ; but it may be that it most truly manifests itself to-day in the readiness with which we bow to new truths as they come from the scholars, the teachers, to whom the inspiration of the Almighty giveth understanding. If a man should try to show it in the way good men did of old, — by covering himself with tow-cloth, sitting on an ash-heap, and disfiguring his person, — we should send him straightway to Worcester or Somerville ; and, if he began to "rend his garments," it would suggest the need of a strait-jacket.

Our rocky New England and old rocky Judæa always seem to have a kind of yearning for each other : Jerusalem governs Massachusetts, and Massachusetts would like to colonize Jerusalem.

> " The pine-tree dreameth of the palm,
>   The palm-tree of the pine."

But political freedom inevitably generates a new type of religious character, as the conclave that contemplates endowing a dotard with infallibility has found out, we trust, before this time.[1] The American of to-day may challenge for himself the noble frankness in his highest relations which did honor to the courage of the Father of the Faithful.

And he may well ask, in view of the slavish beliefs which have governed so large a part of Christendom, whether it was an ascent or a descent from the Roman's

Si fractus illabatur orbis
Impavidum ferient ruinæ

to the monk's

Quid sum miser tunc facturus,
Quem patronum rogaturus ?

Who can help asking such questions as he sits in the light of those blazing windows of the ritual *renaissance*, burning with hectic

---

[1] We have since discovered that the dogma was a foregone conclusion.

colors like the leaves of the decaying forest before the wind has swept it bare, and listens to the delicious strains of the quartet as it carols forth its smiling devotions?

Our dwellings are built on the shell-heaps, the kitchen-middens of the age of stone. Inherited beliefs, as obscure in their origin as the parentage of the cave-dwellers, are stronger with many minds than the evidence of the senses and the simplest deductions of the intelligence. Persons outside of Bedlam can talk of the " dreadful depravity of lunatics," — the sufferers whom we have learned to treat with the tenderest care, as the most to be pitied of all God's children.[1] Mr. Gosse can believe that a fossil skeleton, with the remains of food in its interior, was never part of a living creature, but was made just as we find it,[2] — a kind of stage-property, a

---

[1] Brit. and Foreign Med. Review for July, 1841; Wigan, *op. cit.*

[2] Owen, in Encyc. Brit., art. " Paleontology," p. 124, *note.*

clever cheat, got up by the great Manager of the original Globe Theatre. All we can say of such persons is, that their "illative sense," to use Dr. Newman's phrase, seems to most of us abnormal and unhealthy. We cannot help looking at them as affected with a kind of mental Daltonism.

"Believing ignorance," said an old Scotch divine, "is much better than rash and presumptuous knowledge."[1] But which is most likely to be presumptuous, — ignorance, or knowledge? True faith and true philosophy ought to be one; and those disputes, — *à double vérité,* — those statements, "true according to philosophy, and false according to faith," condemned by the last Council of Lateran,[2] ought not to find a place in the records of an age like our own. Yet so enlightened a philosopher as Faraday could say in a letter to one of his correspondents, "I claim an absolute

---

[1] Buckle, Hist. of Civilization, ii. 327, *note.*

[2] Leibnitz: Consid. sur la Doctrine d'un Esprit Universel.

7

distinction between a religious and an ordinary belief. If I am reproached for weakness in refusing to apply those mental operations, which I think good in high things, to the very highest, I am content to bear the reproach."

We must bestir ourselves; for the new generation is upon us, — the marrow-bone-splitting descendants of the old cannibal troglodytes. Civilized as well as savage races live upon their parents and grandparents. Each generation strangles and devours its predecessor. The young Feejeean carries a cord in his girdle for his father's neck; the young American, a string of propositions or syllogisms in his brain to finish the same relative. The old man says, " Son, I have swallowed and digested the wisdom of the past." The young man says, " Sire, I proceed to swallow and digest thee with all thou knowest." There never was a sand-glass, nor a clepsydra, nor a horologe, that counted the hours and days and years with such terrible significance as this academic chronograph which has just completed a revolution. The prologue of life is finished here at twenty : then come five acts of a decade each, and the play is over, with now and then a pleasant or a tedious afterpiece, when half the lights are put out, and half the orchestra is gone.

We have just seen a life finished whose whole compass was included within the remembered years of many among us. Why was our great prose-minstrel mourned by nations, and buried with kings ? Not merely because of that genius, prolific as Nature herself, we might almost say, in types of character, and aspects of life, whom, for this sufficient reason, we dare to name in connection with the great romancer of the North, and even with the supreme poet of mankind, — was he not a kind of Shakspeare, working in terra-cotta instead of marble ? — but because he vindicated humanity, not against its Maker, but against itself; because he took the part of his frail, erring, sorrowing, dying fellow-creature, against the demonologists who had pretended to write the history of human nature, with a voice that touched the heart as no other had done since the Scotch peasant was laid down to slumber in the soil his song had hallowed.[1]

We are not called to mourn over the frailties of the great story-teller, as we must sorrow in remembering those of the sweet singer of Scotland.   But we all need forgiveness ; and there must be generous failings in every true manhood which it makes Heaven itself happier to pardon.   " I am very human," Dickens said to me one of the last times I ever met him.   And so I feel as if

---

[1] Providence has arranged an admirable system of compensations in the distribution of talents and instincts : so that, as in the rule of three, the product of the extremes of belief equals that of the middle terms; or, as in the astatic needles, the opposite polar forces are balanced against each other. In Scotland, the creed is the Westminster Confession, and the national poet is Burns.   In England, Bunyan stands at one end of the shelf, and Dickens at the other.

I might repeat, in tender remembrance of
Charles Dickens, a few of the lines I wrote
some years ago as my poor tribute to the
memory of Robert Burns : —

> We praise him, not for gifts divine;
>   His Muse was born of woman;
> His manhood breathes in every line:
>   Was ever heart more human ?
>
> We love him, praise him, just for this, —
>   In every form and feature,
> Through wealth and want, through woe and bliss,
>   He saw his fellow-creature.
>
> Ay, Heaven had set one living man
>   Beyond the pedant's tether:
> His virtues, frailties, He may scan
>   Who weighs them all together.

www.ingramcontent.com/pod-product-compliance
Lightning Source LLC
Chambersburg PA
CBHW031455030726
47493CB00030BB/2711